# CRICKET BOY

# CRICKET BOY

A CHINESE TALE RETOLD BY
## FEENIE ZINER
## ILLUSTRATED BY ED YOUNG

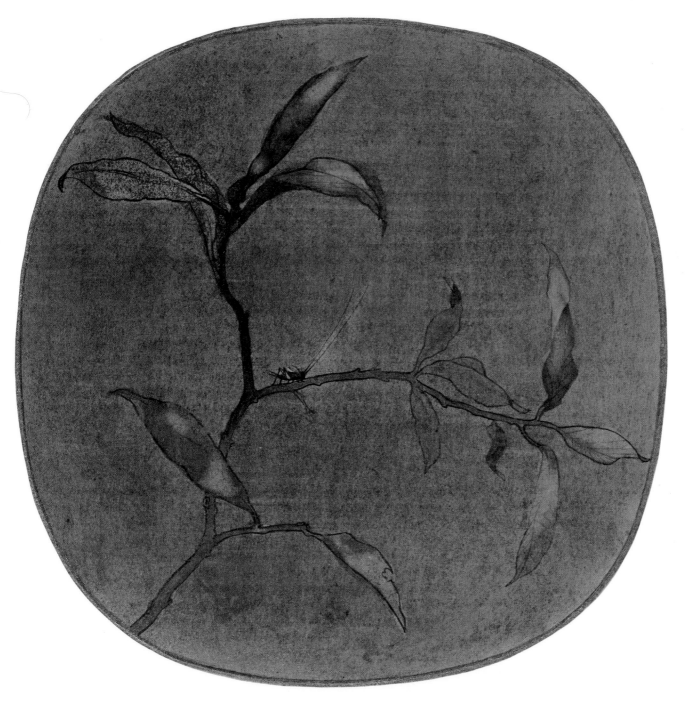

DOUBLEDAY & COMPANY, INC., GARDEN CITY, NEW YORK

For Jane

Library of Congress Catalog Card Number 76-51999
ISBN 0-385-12506-2 Trade
0-385-12507-0 Prebound

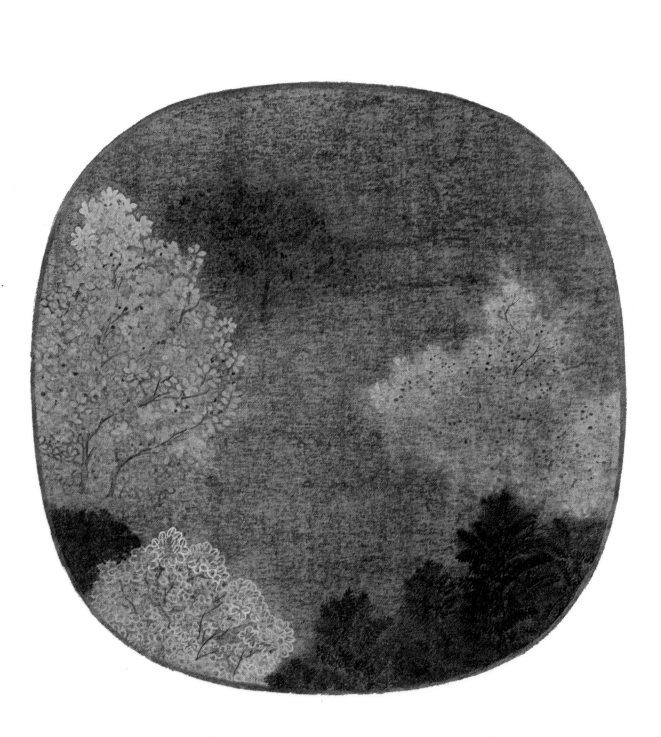

Long ago, in the village of Yung Ping, there lived a scholar by the name of Hu. While everyone else in the village labored in the fields or spread nets in the river to catch fish, Scholar Hu sat at a low table in his little house, considering large questions. Day in and day out he searched the ancient chronicles, the great books of Chinese wisdom, looking for the answers to difficult problems. "How can great things grow from small ones?" And, "How does power spring from weakness?" No one in the village thought it odd that Scholar Hu should spend his days in study, for in China a man of learning was respected above all others, even if he was poor.

Scholar Hu was very poor indeed. Four times he had taken examinations for a government post, and four times he had failed. For while he tried to concentrate on difficult problems, his mind was full of concern for his motherless son, Hu Sing. Were it not for the pittance the boy earned, helping in the

fields, Hu Sing, his grandmother, and Scholar Hu himself would have perished of poverty. Yet above all else, Scholar Hu wanted his son to become a man of wisdom. He wanted Hu Sing to bring honor, in his turn, to the name of the Family Hu. The fear that his child might live out his life in ignorance gnawed at the heart of Scholar Hu.

Of course, Scholar Hu could have taught Hu Sing much that he knew himself. But Hu Sing was a child. He was not interested in large questions. He did not like to sit perfectly still, learning to hold his brush just so, just exactly so, in order to inscribe beautiful words on paper. When his work in the fields was over and the evening meal was done, Hu Sing wanted to play with his crickets. He saved the best crumbs for them. He wove little cages for them, out of straw. He named them lovingly: One-leg King, Big Head, Cripple Prince. He longed to own a true champion, a cricket that would pursue an opponent around the fighting bowl and overturn him with one bold thrust.

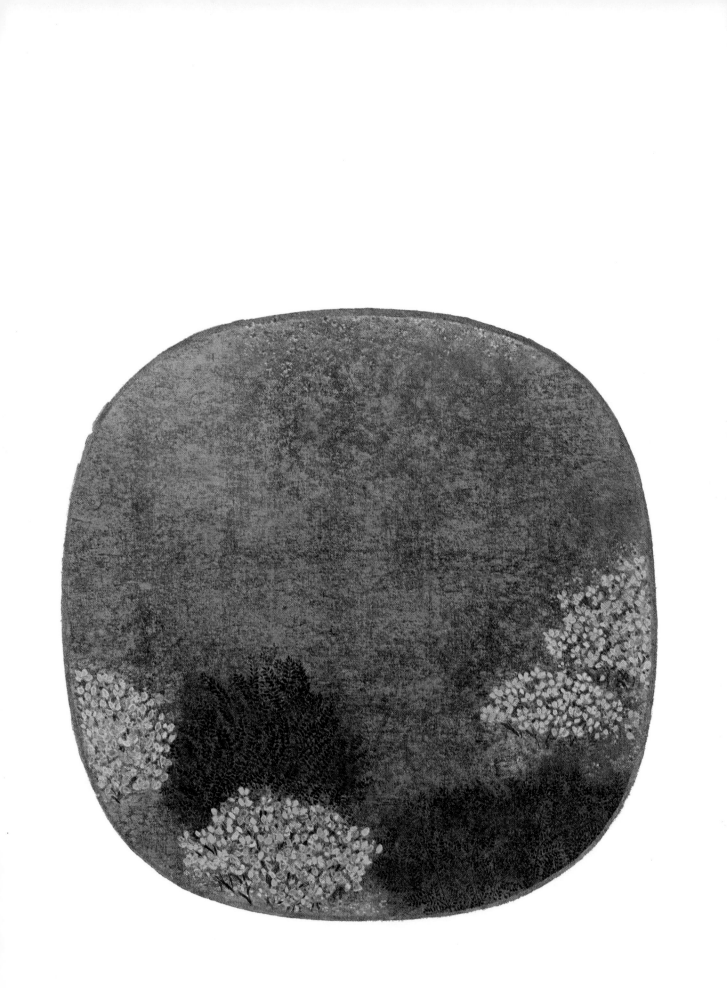

One evening Hu Sing sat on the floor of the little house, carving a tickling rod with which to prod his fighters into battle. His father watched the boy, admiring the skill and care with which he worked. And a new question came into his mind: "Is there not as great a mystery in the life of a cricket as there is in the life of Man?" That question led to others: "How is it that some crickets are naturally shy, and others are born fighters? What happens to the spirit of a cricket when summer ends, and its body dies?"

These thoughts were so interesting to him that he resolved that, since his son would not interest himself in scholarly matters, he would interest himself in crickets.

Hu Sing was delighted. Together, they spent hours in the garden, listening for crickets. "You must learn to keep yourself perfectly still, my son," the father said, "for the catcher of crickets must be silent and swift, and not too proud to kneel before the smallest creature." Once, Hu Sing brought his

father a new cricket and his father said, "See, my son, this is a female. If you wish her to fight, you will have to keep her children with her." Another time, Hu Sing caught a cricket with a very loud chirp. "The loudest chirper often sings only to keep his courage up. Listen, instead, for the quiet fellows. There you will find true pride."

Scholar Hu observed the lives of crickets so carefully that, in time, he himself had the finest collection of crickets in the district, and his fame spread far and wide. He kept his champion, Black Dragon, in a jar upon his desk. Black Dragon was a broad-shouldered, strong-legged cricket whose cheerful chirp gave Scholar Hu heart to continue with his studies. When he felt gloomy and discouraged, he had only to lift the top of the cricket jar. The moment his body was touched by light, Black Dragon sprang into the hand of Scholar Hu. "So it will be with Hu Sing," thought the scholar. "Someday I shall pass my examinations. Someday I shall be able to send Hu Sing to school. It is never too late for

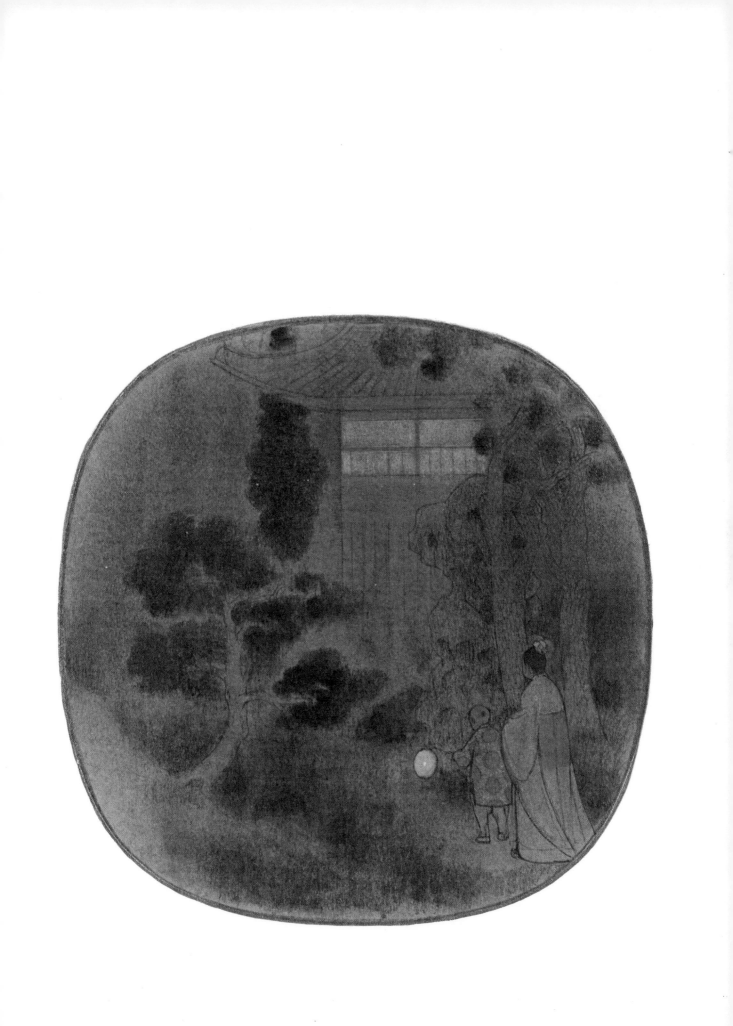

learning. The moment the light of scholarship touches his mind, Hu Sing will begin to grow into a man of wisdom. He will carry on the name of the Family Hu. He will do honor to our ancestors."

One day, when the sky gods had moved into the third quarter, Scholar Hu was sitting at his low table, trying to write a poem in praise of crickets. Fishermen were hauling in their nets and farmers were returning from the fields when a courier galloped into the dusty square of Yung Ping. The village magistrate, an idle fellow, bustled out in his underwear to greet him.

"Stand back! Go away!" he shouted to the women who rushed out of their houses, still carrying their soup ladles, to stare at the stranger. "Can't you see that this man brings an important message for me?"

But the courier did not dismount. He leaned over his saddle and said, "Direct me, O Fat One, to the house of the Scholar Hu."

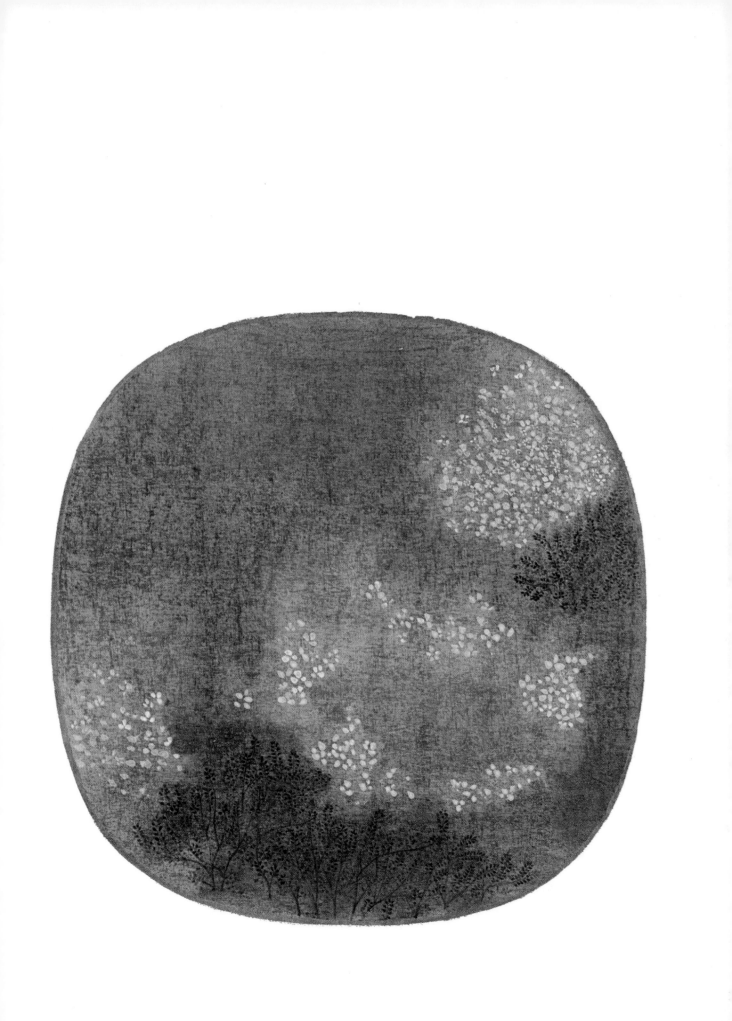

"The Scholar Hu? What do you want with him? *I* am the chief official of Yung Ping. *I* am the person for whom your message must be intended. Unless, of course," he added with an unpleasant chuckle, "unless, of course, it's a cricket you want. If it's a cricket, Scholar Hu might be of some help to you."

"I come to summon Scholar Hu to the palace of the Emperor," the courier said. "The Emperor wishes a cricket match."

All the villagers gasped. Such an honor had not befallen anyone in Yung Ping in the memory of the oldest person in the town. Everyone crowded about the courier, offering to lead him to the little house near the river where Scholar Hu lived with his son and with the child's grandmother. But Hu Sing, whose head barely reached the underbelly of the courier's horse, darted ahead of them and cried in a piercing voice, "Baba! Baba! The Emperor sends for you!"

"You leap about like a cricket full of red-pepper seed!" the father said, placing a gentle hand on the overheated head of his son.

"But, Baba! A courier has come! The Emperor wishes you to put Black Dragon into the fighting bowl against his own champion!"

Scholar Hu felt faint. The Emperor Hwie Jung prized his crickets above all else on earth. Since he kept only winners in his collection, the cricket cages of the Emperor contained champions among champions.

At the same time, Scholar Hu realized that this was the most important thing to happen in Yung Ping in centuries. No one would ever again mention the name of the Family Hu without adding, ". . . whose cricket fought the Emperor's." His eyes filled with tears.

"Surely," he said to his son, "this is a sign of a blessed intervention on our behalf, by the ancestors of the Family Hu."

The boy did not need to be told that only hunger and poverty had prevented his father from passing his examinations. That their ancestors should have spoken to the spirit world on behalf of his father

seemed a natural kindness and concern for the man he loved so dearly. And so, even before the courier reached the little house near the river, father and son made plans to offer thanks at the family altar in the garden behind the house, to salute the Hus of the past who guarded and blessed their humble lives.

While the entire village assembled in front of the little house, the courier instructed Scholar Hu to prepare himself for the journey to the court. The following day, he said, a boat bearing the Emperor's seal would arrive on the river, to carry him to the palace. The crowd parted to admit Hu Pai, the mother of Scholar Hu, who hobbled along behind the others so that she might hear the good news from her son. Ever since his wife had died, good fortune had been an infrequent visitor to the household. Yet even as the old woman embraced the scholar with joy, the fat magistrate waddled up and said, "Scholar Hu, you are bringing a great misfortune upon our village."

"How so?" inquired Scholar Hu, drawing both his mother and his son closer to him.

"If your cricket should defeat the Emperor's, he will be angry. His troops might come and destroy the village."

"You are joking," Scholar Hu replied with a smile. Everyone knew that there were many districts in the Middle Kingdom in which officials overtaxed the poor, and drought and flood and disease made existence terrible, while the Emperor Hwie Jung absorbed himself in cricket fighting. "He rules best who rules least," was the Emperor's philosophy.

"The Emperor is not a bandit," said Scholar Hu mildly. "He merely wishes a cricket match. Besides," he added, "Black Dragon might lose!"

"What do you know of the behavior of Emperors?" demanded the magistrate. "If his cricket loses to yours, he may chop off your head and hang it on the palace wall. Who, then, would care for your son?"

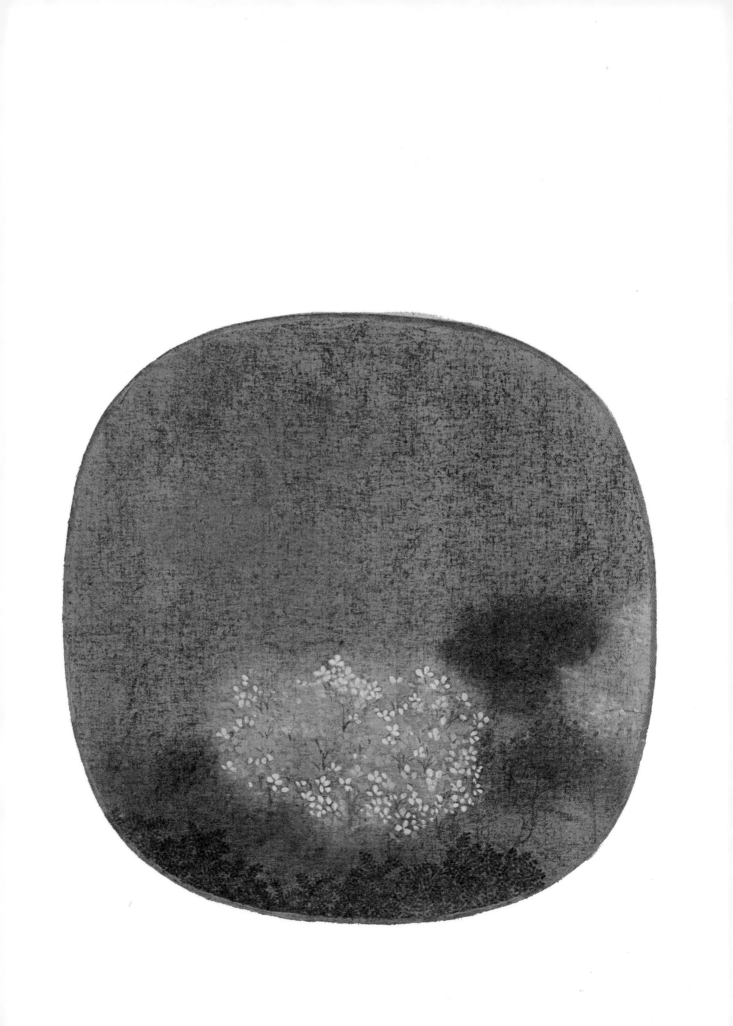

"What would you suggest?" asked Scholar Hu.

The magistrate leaned forward and whispered in Scholar Hu's ear. "You cannot put us all in such danger, I tell you!" he concluded.

But a great murmur arose from the villagers, who had lived together so long that they were as one family in their feeling for Scholar Hu, the most learned man among them. "The village of Yung Ping will attain great honor," they said. "Scholar Hu must go."

When the crowd about the door finally thinned, Scholar Hu placed his hand on Hu Sing's head. "Fear not, my son," he said, "all will be well. Our ancestors have blessed us, truly. Black Dragon will not fail."

Together with Hu Pai, Scholar Hu and Hu Sing knelt before the graves of their ancestors and asked that the spirit world look with kindness upon the coming trial.

But Hu Sing was frightened by the magistrate's words. The magistrate always scowled when the

villagers bowed low before his father. Only the day before, the magistrate had shaken his fist at Hu Sing. He and the magistrate's son had put their crickets into the fighting bowl, and Hu Sing's second-stringer, Cripple Prince, had overturned the older boy's best fighter, even though it was full of pepper.

"Suppose," thought Hu Sing, "suppose the magistrate does harm to my father's champion?" He knew it was a foolish fear, yet it filled his mind. While his father and his grandmother spoke to a kindly neighbor who offered the loan of a dusty cloak for the journey to the Emperor's palace, Hu Sing slipped into the house. His heart beat like a drum. He drew the cricket jar to the edge of his father's table. His arms were scarcely long enough to reach the top. Carefully he lifted off the lid. Black Dragon jumped out. In his haste to catch him, Hu Sing knocked over the jar, and it crashed to the floor, right into the shadows where Black Dragon crouched. Alas, the jar broke the big cricket's back!

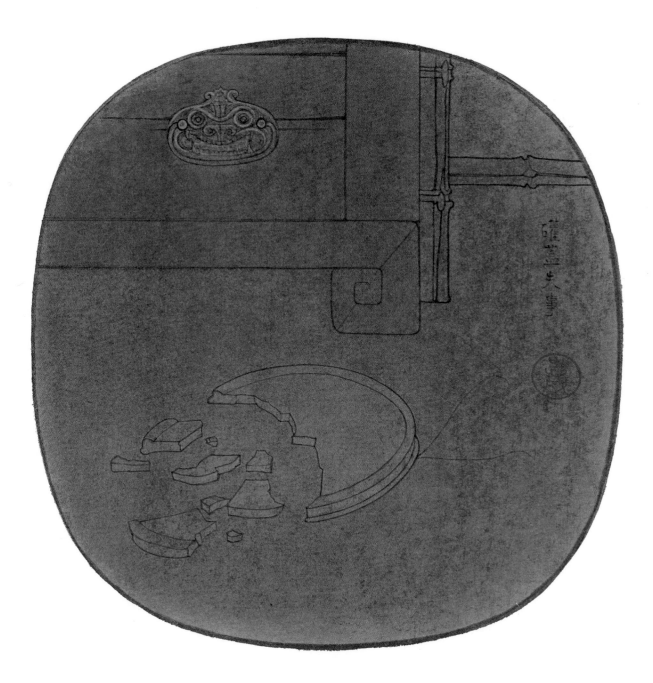

Hu Sing felt the blow as if it had fallen upon him. Tenderly he picked up the champion, and whispered, "Black Dragon, don't die! Don't die!" But Black Dragon waved his feelers in a final farewell and lay motionless in the little boy's hand.

It was the end of Hu Sing's world. With trembling hands he placed the lifeless cricket on his father's table and, silent as a shadow, he fled across the garden, past the graves, through the grassy fields to the riverbank.

The village fool, thinking that the great splash he heard might be a fish, lifted his net from the river and drew out the limp body of Hu Sing. Howling with anguish, he carried the child to his father's house. "We rejoiced too soon!" cried Hu Pai, in horror. When Scholar Hu saw the body of the cricket on his table, he understood what had happened and his grief knew no bounds.

Tenderly he took the child and placed him on his bed. He knelt at his side, hoping for some sign of

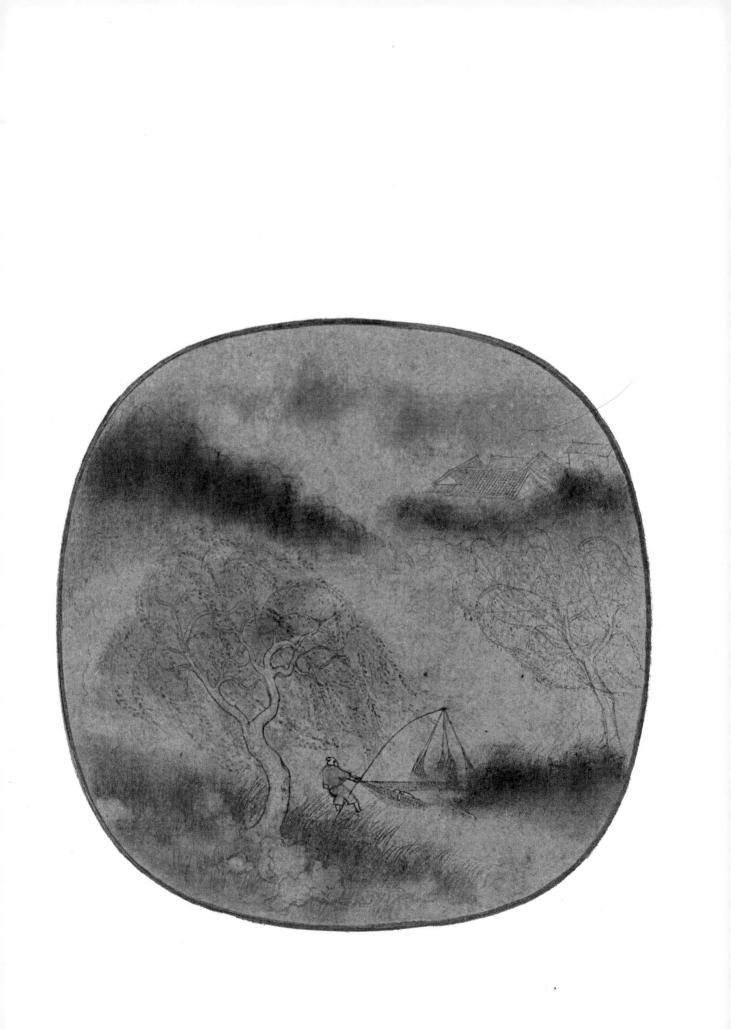

life, but the child was in a coma so deep that it seemed he would never awaken. Gladly would he have given his own life to restore his son's, but hope vanished like the lost light of day. Hu Pai brewed infusions of tea, held a glass under Hu Sing's nose for a sign of breath, felt his pulse. To no avail. At last she lit a candle and placed it above the child's head.

When word reached the magistrate, he hurried over to the house of Scholar Hu for a second time. Scholar Hu did not withdraw his gaze from his son. The magistrate shuffled his feet, cleared his throat, and said, "I am sorry your son is dead, Scholar Hu." The grieving man did not reply.

"But I was thinking: I was wrong when I said you ought not to go to the palace. If the Emperor finds out that someone in the village of Yung Ping killed a champion cricket, he might punish us all with a heavy tax. I ask you, Scholar Hu: take another cricket to the court tomorrow. As for your son's funeral, seven days must pass before his soul

comes to rest. Exactly enough time for your journey to the court and back. It works out perfectly. You will be back here just in time. In appreciation, the village will pay for Hu Sing's coffin. Well? What do you say?''

Scholar Hu said nothing, but continued to kneel beside the body of his son. There was nothing for the magistrate to do but to take his leave, which he did, feeling that he had been more than generous to Scholar Hu.

For hours, Scholar Hu and his mother, Hu Pai, knelt beside the body of Hu Sing. At length the father spoke. "Go to bed, my dear mother. I shall watch the child." The poor old woman dragged herself away on her little feet. "Ai, that such a sorrow should befall me in my old age!" she murmured.

Now the father was alone with his sorrow. Neither human breath nor cricket song relieved the silence. Just before midnight the poor man's head drooped upon his breast. He dreamed that his dead

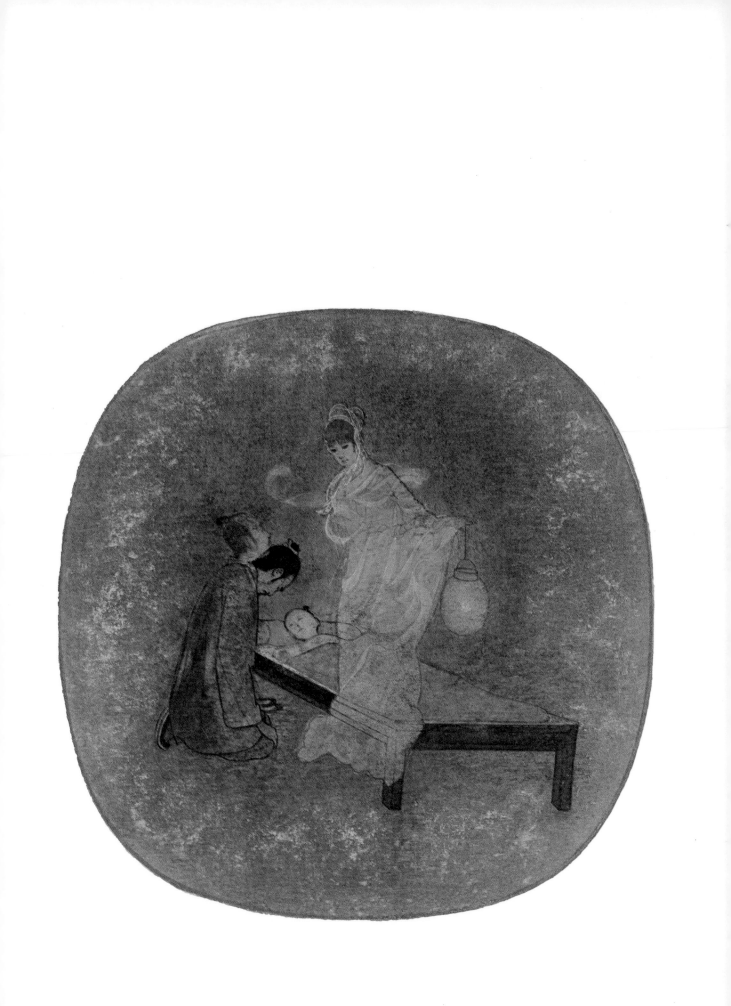

wife came into the room and pointed to a rock in his garden—a rock he knew as well as his inkstand. Startled by the vividness of his vision, Scholar Hu arose, took the candle, and went out into the garden. The sky shimmered like a river of stars. From under the very rock he'd seen in his dream came a fine high chirp—one long, clear note that made the scholar's heart turn over. He marked the rock with a drop of wax from his candle and returned to his vigil at Hu Sing's bedside.

As soon as the dragons of day fired the earth's rim, he went once more into the garden, and lifted the rock, and a little cricket jumped right up into his hand. How beautifully shaped it was! But how tiny! It had two reddish marks on its head, at the base of its feelers; a tiny gold stripe crossed the top of its neck; its wings were an iridescent green.

Scholar Hu took it indoors and tested it against Hu Sing's second-stringers. The tiny cricket defeated them, one after another. Never before had Scholar Hu seen a cricket with such determination,

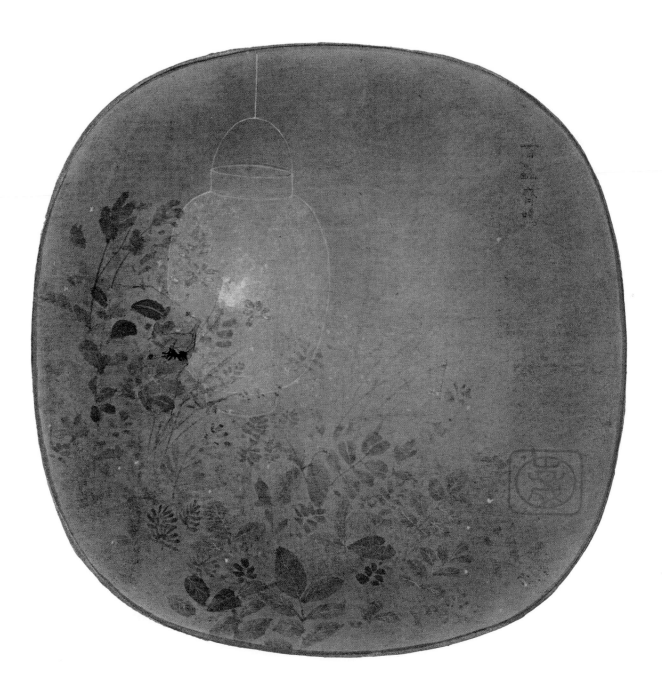

such strategy. This little cricket had a powerful will of its own.

So, when the river boat bearing the Emperor's seal arrived the following day, Scholar Hu was ready. Once more he knelt beside the pale, silent body of his little son. He gazed at Hu Pai with a question in his eyes. "Do you think, my son, that I shall leave his bedside for a moment, when you are gone?" she asked. "I, who have cared for the boy every day of his life, since his beloved mother left us?" Scholar Hu nodded and embraced the old woman. Everyone in the village followed him down to the landing stage, even the magistrate, to wish him well.

Scholar Hu passed through the great gates of the Emperor's palace without seeing them. He took no notice of the huge stone lions that guarded the stairway leading up to the Imperial abode.

The Commissioner in Charge of Cricket Fights hurried across the courtyard to greet him. Like all

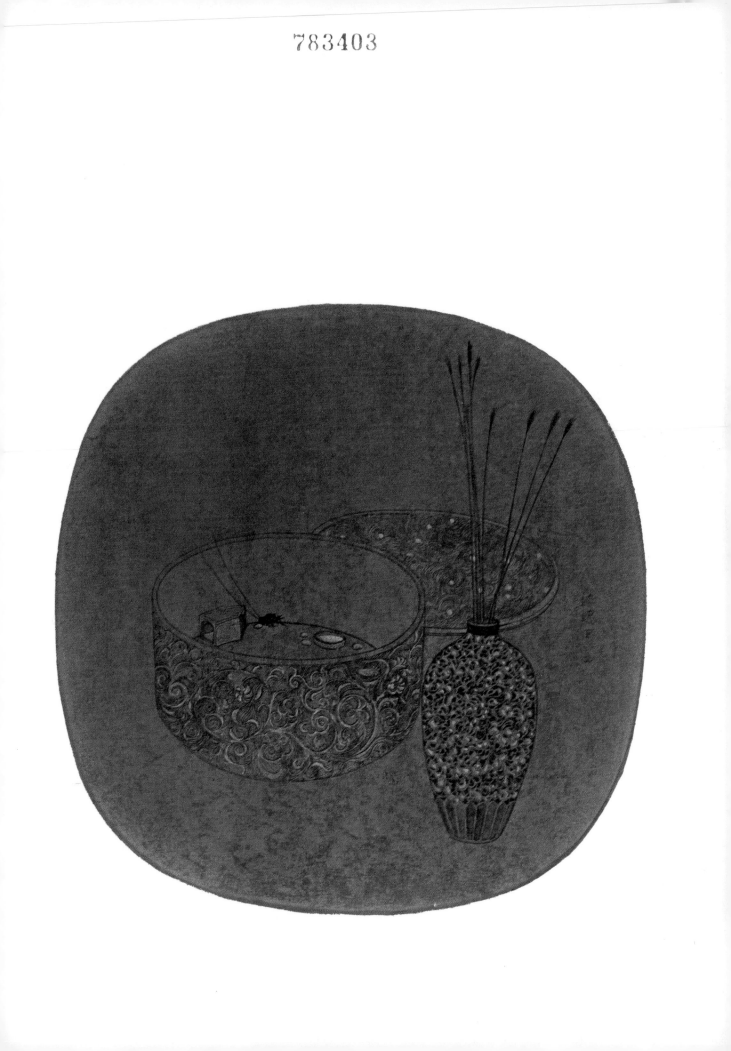

gentlemen of means and refinement, he carried his own favorite cricket with him in a woven cage, attached to his belt.

"The match will take place tomorrow," the commissioner said, and led Scholar Hu toward the chamber in which the Emperor's crickets lived. The cages were lined with costly silk. Tiny dishes for the crickets' food and water hung from their sides. The fighting bowl was set in rosewood and inlaid with gold and ivory of intricate design. The Emperor's crickets were well chosen: broad-shouldered, strong-legged creatures, ready on the instant to leap into battle, to chase their opponents around the bowl, to seize them with their powerful pincers and hurl them on their backs or to force them out of the bowl, either of which would signify victory.

Scholar Hu tried to imagine the Emperor in his splendid clothes, crouching in his garden, kneeling in the grass, humbling himself before so tiny a creature, but he could not.

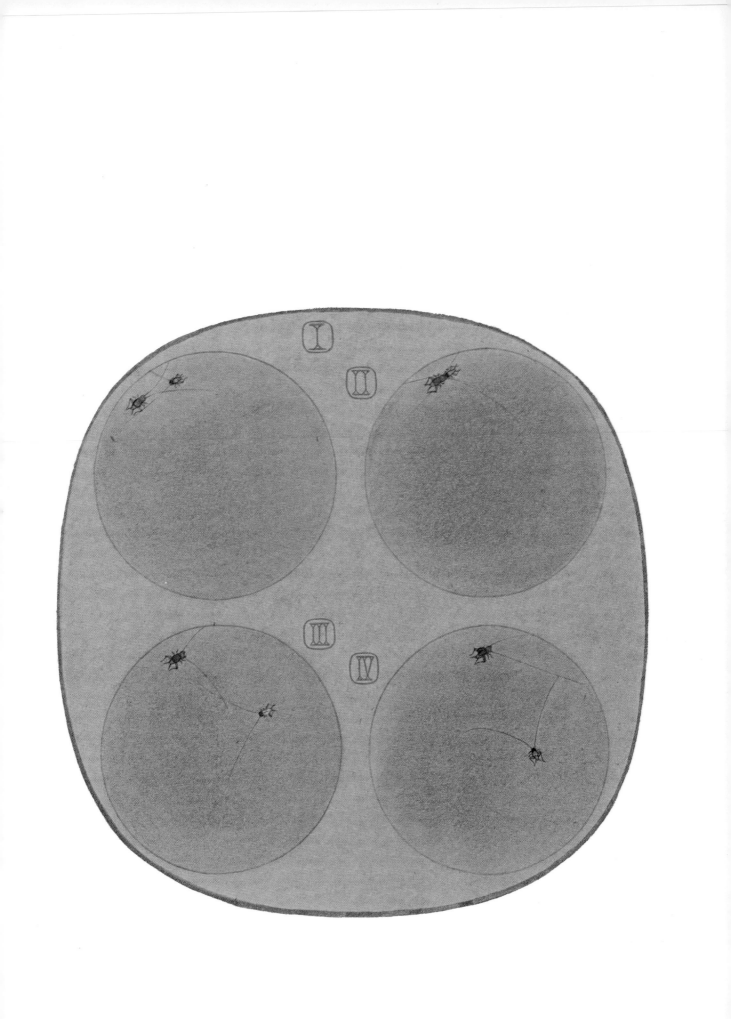

Next morning there was great excitement at the court, for the Emperor, who preferred cricket fighting to all other entertainment, would speak of nothing else. When the gong in the courtyard sounded noon, only two men entered the great room in which the match was to be held: the Emperor, and Scholar Hu. Beside the fighting bowl lay the tickling sticks. Each man placed a cricket in the bowl and bent to watch.

The Emperor picked up his tickling stick and touched the tail of his champion. The big cricket turned swiftly and flipped the nameless little cricket onto its back. "But of course," the Emperor's face said. "Don't I always win?" But before he could declare the match finished, the little cricket righted itself. While the big champion chirped loudly, the little cricket charged, caught the boaster off guard, and chased him all the way up to the lip of the bowl. The spirit of the Emperor's cricket was broken forever. "What a champion!" the Emperor exclaimed, his eyebrows rising under his cap. For he

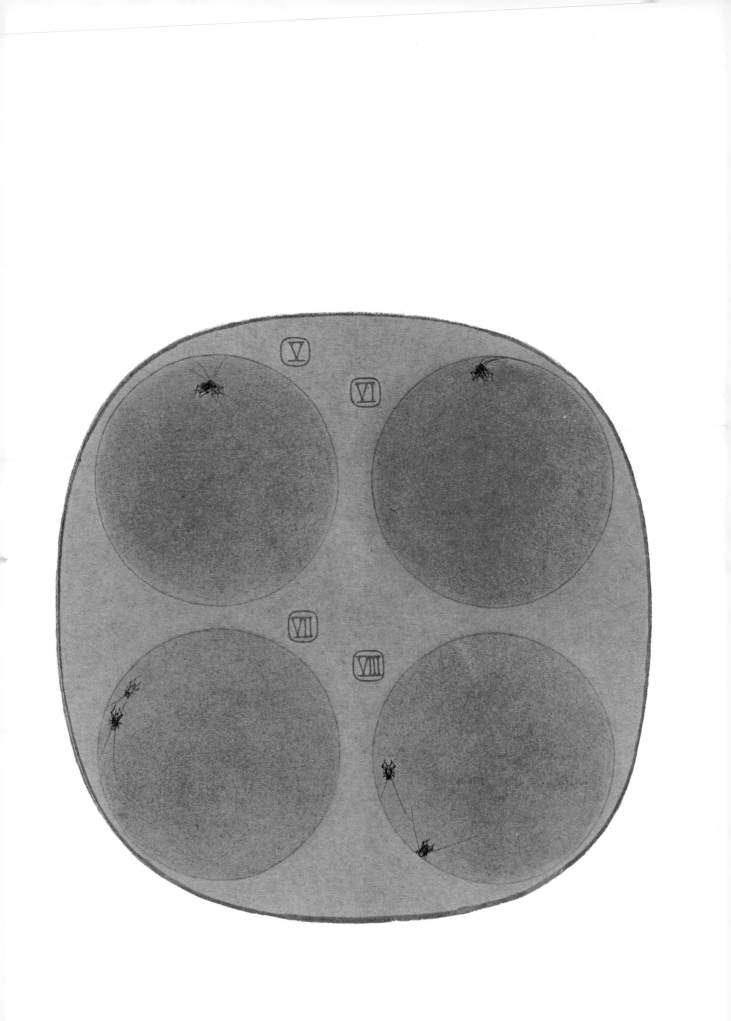

knew that his own cricket would never recover from this sudden defeat.

"Tell me, Scholar Hu," the Emperor said, "what is your wish, that I may reward you?"

Scholar Hu replied with difficulty.

"Alas, most exalted ruler, my only wish is not within your power to grant."

Astounded that this poor man could wish for something so grand that it lay beyond his power, the Emperor leaned forward and inquired, "What can your wish be?"

"I wish that my son might live again," he said. And, in very few words, he told the Emperor that at his journey's end lay the funeral of his only son. All the wealth of the Middle Kingdom would not, now, halt the extinction of the Family Hu.

Scholar Hu departed from the Emperor's palace as empty-handed as he had come. His life had lost all meaning, for, with the death of his son, he was cut off alike from his past and from his future.

People lined both sides of the river as the Emperor's boat carried Scholar Hu home to the village of Yung Ping. No one called aloud to him. They only watched him, knowing his soul was heavy as a rock within him. He nodded to his friends respectfully, and hurried on to his tiny house, close to the river. There Hu Pai still knelt at the side of the child. She lifted her careworn face to her son as Scholar Hu's shadow filled the doorway.

"No sign of life," she said sadly. "But you, my son? How did you fare at the Emperor's palace?"

"My little cricket defeated the Emperor's champion," he replied.

As he spoke these words, the eyelids of Hu Sing fluttered. While his father and grandmother stood as if rooted to the earthen floor, the little boy stirred, then sat up and rubbed his eyes.

"Oh!" he said. "Baba! Grandmother! I have had the strangest dream! I dreamed that I wrestled with the Emperor's general! He was so much bigger than I! There were so many grand people, watching! I was so frightened! But I defeated him!"

That night the whole village of Yung Ping rejoiced. The magistrate himself gave a great feast of thanksgiving. Indeed, that night there was rejoicing as well in Heaven.

But after all the feasting and rejoicing was over, Scholar Hu, lying in his bed, asked himself what had happened. What had *really* happened? And it seemed to him that of all the difficult questions he had ever asked himself, this was the most difficult one of all.

We know as little of the answer as did Scholar Hu.

But the people of Yung Ping still remember the story, and they tell about Hu Sing, the cricket boy, down to this very day.

FEENIE ZINER, who makes her home in Dobbs Ferry, New York, is the author of books for both children and adults. In addition to her own writing, she teaches courses in literature and writing at the University of Connecticut in Storrs, Connecticut.

ED YOUNG has illustrated over ten books for young prople, including Caldecott runner-up *The Emperor and the Kite*, by Jane Yolen. Mr. Young resides in Hastings On Hudson, New York.